F. J. Bramwell

Our Big Guns

F. J. Bramwell

Our Big Guns

ISBN/EAN: 9783337092269

Printed in Europe, USA, Canada, Australia, Japan

Cover: Foto ©Andreas Hilbeck / pixelio.de

More available books at **www.hansebooks.com**

BIRMINGHAM AND MIDLAND INSTITUTE.

"OUR BIG GUNS."

AN ADDRESS

DELIVERED IN THE TOWN HALL, BIRMINGHAM,

On the 20th September, 1886.

BY

SIR FREDERICK BRAMWELL, D.C.L., F.R.S.,

PAST PRESIDENT INST. C.E.,

PRESIDENT.

LONDON:

PRINTED BY WM. CLOWES & SONS, LIMITED,

STAMFORD STREET AND CHARING CROSS.

1886.

ADDRESS

DELIVERED IN THE TOWN HALL, BIRMINGHAM,

On Monday, 20th September, 1886,

By SIR FREDERICK BRAMWELL, D.C.L., F.R.S.,

PAST-PRESIDENT, INSTITUTION OF CIVIL ENGINEERS, ETC., ETC.

"*Thou shalt not covet.*" How simple, how intelligible; how comprehensive—so comprehensive indeed, as (if obeyed) to render unnecessary certain other commandments, one of which is, "Thou shalt not steal," stealing being merely covetousness brought into practice.

Let us for a few minutes, consider, what would be the altered condition of this kingdom, if its inhabitants ceased to covet.

On approaching a large town, what does the traveller commonly see on its outskirts? A pretentious building, frowning like some ancient castle, but turning out to be the gaol. What would he find to be the fact as regards the prisoners? What percentage of the numbers would be confined there, because they acquired by burglary, or by theft, that which they had first coveted?

Some may be awaiting their trial for murder, or even the doom consequent thereon; and this, culminating crime, how often has it grown out of the sin of coveting, resistance to capture when committing a burglary, bringing into use the too

ready revolver, with the result of the householder, or the
policeman shot dead!

But enough of these mournful considerations, which after
all, apply only, to but a small percentage of the population.
Let us for a minute or two consider the advantages in matters
of every-day life which would be attendant on the cessation of
coveting. How improved, would this every-day life be if
individuals would not covet!

Think of the blessing of being sure, that the purchase you
had made, was really the purchase you had intended to make;
that the cotton fabric did not owe its seeming goodness to
flour; that the "all new wool" was not merely shoddy or mungo;
and that the silk was unmixed with cotton; and so on, and
so on.

Frauds such as these are an outcome of covetousness, and
they affect us most nearly, not when practised in connection
with articles such as I have just mentioned, but when they are
practised in the instance of articles of food, which should
sustain our lives, or still worse in the article of medicine, to be
administered to us, as the means of cure, in sickness. To so
great an extent did such frauds prevail, that there was needed
the Adulteration of Food and Drugs Act in 1875, and the
creation of the Public Analyst. Horrible suggestion—our bread,
our milk, our butter, coffee, tea, and wine, our medicine, may
none of them be that which they purport to be, but may be
found by the analyst to be the products of "covetousness,"
aided by "applied science."

Imagine the benefit of being able to dispense with locks,
bolts, and bars, and with the nightly round of visits, to window-
fastenings and to door-locks!

Again, if men ceased to covet, we should get rid of much
sham philanthropy, philanthropy of the Judas character:
" Why was not this ointment sold for three hundred pence, and
" given to the poor?" We are told he said this, "not that he
" cared for the poor; but because he was a thief, and had the
" bag, and bare what was put therein."

In those days it is not an infrequent cry. "Here is an old " Institution; it has large funds; it administers them by a " Master and a Court of Wardens. This must be wrong; " such titles are inconsistent with proper management. The " funds should be administered by a Commission, with a first " Commissioner, a second Commissioner, a first Assistant Com- " missioner, a second Assistant-Commissioner, a Secretary and a " staff of Clerks, all 10 to 4 men, and all paid." Useless to prove that the accusations are unfounded, that the trusts have been most liberally carried out; that the non-trust funds have been as wisely used as they might have been by a high-minded Christian gentleman, a philanthropist in the true sense of the word. All useless. The spirit of Judas' covetousness is there, and the spirit of the old lying excuse is there; it probably will not take the shape of giving to the poor, but some suggestion of an altered use will be made; the true motive, however, will be covetousness.

I do not mean to say, that if the individuals making up the community, were all fully obedient to the commandment, we should thereby be without crime, or that gaols and policemen could be dispensed with, but I do say that there would be an enormous diminution in crime, accompanied by a corresponding reduction in the cost of repression, and that the increased en-joyment of life would be such, as we cannot even succeed in picturing to ourselves.

Great however, as would be the blessings to any nation, if the individuals forming it were to cease to covet, these blessings would be far exceeded, by those which would accrue to mankind at large, if the nations themselves ceased to covet.

Ships of war, armies, militia, volunteers, all the preparations for defence, would be needless, and would therefore cease.

Cease also would the conscription, which falls so heavily on many a population, and so hardly on particular individuals of those populations. The highest talent, the greatest ability, the utmost industry applied to the support of those most needing it, are all in the eyes of the conscription of no importance; provided the lad is sound in wind and limb, and can pull a trigger when he is told, and stand to be shot at, it matters not whether his mental powers are those of an ignorant peasant, or those of a Newton.

As with the sham philanthropy among individuals, so would it be with the sham philanthropy of nations.

A State that covets a slice of the territory of another, hardly ever has the hardihood to avow it. An excuse is found, such as, that some section of its population is oppressed, and war must be made in order to relieve it. The usual result of such a war being to leave this particular section, quite as much oppressed as before, with the addition of the general oppression of the rest of the nation, and this state of things continues, until the conqueror is bought off by the cession of the coveted territory, the true object for which the war was initiated.

Any excuse will suffice; liberty itself may be invoked as the excuse for inflicting bondage; we know that at the end of the last century, nations were invaded and despoiled in order to confer on them the blessings of (the so-called) Liberty, Equality, Fraternity; thus anticipating on a wholesale scale the conduct suggested by some wags among our American friends, who say, when speaking of themselves, " Our country is the freest country in the world; every man does as he likes, and if he does'nt, we make him."

We know that if this, our England, were to disarm to-day, not a year would elapse, before we should find ourselves under the rule of some kind neighbour, who would assure us that the occupation of our country, was not by any means due to the coveting of our possessions, but arose from the warmest interest in our welfare, and that it was done entirely for our good.

It is a remarkable thing, however, that nations do not like the good that is thus done to them; moreover, it is a duty to keep temptation out of the way of those who are too susceptible to its influence; on these grounds we arm—to protect ourselves, and to keep covetous thoughts out of the minds of others.

In these days we "arm" with so many weapons of offence, and means of defence, that a mere enumeration of them, would occupy nearly the whole time at our disposal, and would be but of little profit. I think we may be far better employed, in considering some one special weapon, with such matters as are ancillary to its use, or as are the objects of its attack.

It might be expected, having regard to the locality, that in making a selection among our weapons, I should have chosen small arms for my subject, for the manufacture of which arms this town of Birmingham has so high a reputation ; but I propose to address you on the very opposite of small arms, namely, on " Big Guns," and of necessity in connection therewith, I must say something about the powder and projectiles with which these guns are charged, and about the armour they are designed to attack.

In speaking of Big Guns I propose to omit all early history, not to take up your time by reference to guns made of staves and hooped, nor even to describe the manufacture of the cast-iron cannon such as were used at the time of the Crimean War—whether those made by casting a solid cylinder and boring it out, or those produced according to the early specification for cannon cast hollow, which instructed the manufacturer to proceed as follows :—

" Take a long cylindrical hole, put it upright in the mould, " and run your metal round about it."

These directions are clear, but I fear that apparently simple and inexpensive as the process is, there would be found considerable difficulty in carrying it out.

Although I do not propose to describe the manufacture of obsolete weapons, I find that I must (in order to introduce the existing construction) ask your attention for a short time to the value of the guns (and of their charges) with which Nelson fought, to attack unarmoured wooden ships, guns that remained up to within the last thirty years. A cast-iron muzzle-loader, rarely exceeding on shipboard a calibre of 6·3 inches, a length of bore of 9 feet, or 17 calibres, and a weight of 56 cwt. This gun had a smooth (i. e. unrifled) bore, of uniform diameter from end to end, and fired a spherical shot of 32 lbs. weight.

If solid shot were used, you will see the weight was incapable of adjustment, being determined by that of a sphere of cast iron of a diameter slightly less than that of the bore, the difference being to allow the " windage " that the irregularity of the surface of the projectile rendered necessary.

The charge of powder was commonly about one-third of the weight of the ball.

To come to more modern guns of the same construction ; take as an example the 68-pounder, the heaviest gun it was thought possible, at the date of its use, to mount on shipboard ; this was an 8-inch gun, the length of its bore was 9 feet 6 inches or 14¼ calibres, the weight of the gun was 95 cwt., the charge of powder was 16 lbs., and the velocity of the 68 lb. ball on leaving the muzzle was about 1600 feet per second.

It will be seen that as the bore of the gun and the weight of the ball increased, it was deemed expedient not to retain the relative proportion of powder to ball, viz. one-third, that had prevailed in the 32-pounder, but to reduce it to a little below one-fourth. Neither was it found that the same length in calibres could be given, and these were reduced from the 17 in the 32-pounder to 14¼ in the 68-pounder.

It will be clear to you, that as a shot passes through the air its velocity must gradually diminish, and it will also be clear to you that as the velocity diminishes, the stored up energy in the shot, or the power to do work, upon that which it is to strike, also diminishes. This it does indeed in a ratio far exceeding that of the mere reduction in velocity, viz. in the ratio of the squares, so that a shot that is still travelling, at half the pace of the muzzle velocity, contains only one-fourth of the energy that was stored up in it as it left the mouth of the gun, and possesses therefore only one-fourth of the destructive power. But there is another reason why the retention as far as possible of the muzzle velocity is of importance, which is, that it enables a longer range to be obtained, and shorter ranges to be accomplished with less elevation of the gun—a great advantage, as the following considerations will show. If the velocity were infinite, so that the effect of gravity could not come into play, the gun could be laid point blank on the object to be hit, and we should then get far better shooting than we get now, wonderfully good as that shooting is. But owing to the necessity of giving the gun elevation, varying with the velocity and the range distance, the success of the shot at long ranges is sadly dependent on the powder; a little difference in the moisture, for example, may cause the shot to exceed the normal velocity, or to fall off therefrom by a few feet per second, with the result that in passing along the curved line of flight, which the combination of the gun's elevation and the action of gravity has imposed on it, it is submitted to this action of gravity for more or less time, and the shot will therefore either pitch beyond, or fall short of the exact spot intended to be hit.

Now it is obvious that the form of the projectile must have a great influence upon the question, whether or not the muzzle velocity shall be rapidly diminished, or shall be fairly maintained. No one can doubt that if there were two bodies of equal weight, one made in the form of a javelin and the other in that of a flat disc, and if both were cast from the hand with equal velocities, the disc being propelled flatways against the air, that the javelin would retain at the end of a given time, much more of its initial velocity, than would be retained by the disc. Similarly with the projectile.

To revert to the 68 lb. 8-inch sphere with its muzzle velocity of 1600 feet per second: at the end of 500 yards of flight this velocity would have fallen to 1200 feet, and at the end of 1000 yards it would possess a velocity of only 950 feet. But if we were to adopt the javelin principle, even although we made a very blunt one, viz. if we were to put our 68 lbs. into the form of a cylinder (with a Gothic arch-shaped head) having a diameter of 5 inches with an extreme length of about 15 inches, the muzzle velocity of 1600 feet would at 500 yards be 1480 feet, and at 1000 yards would be 1360 feet.

But another advantage would ensue from disposing this weight of metal into the form of a long small cylinder, instead of into that of a sphere, which is, that although the energies of a sphere and of a cylinder of equal weight, and having equal velocities, would be the same, in the case of the cylinder the energy would be concentrated upon a smaller surface, thereby increasing the intensity of attack upon each unit of area of the surface struck ; in fact, the same cause that enables the long projectile to cleave the air in a manner superior to that in which the spherical projectile can pass through it, enables the long projectile to penetrate a solid resistance more readily than it can be penetrated by the sphere—an imperative reason for adopting the elongated form when it is remembered, that the object to be penetrated (when attacking a ship) is no longer wood, but is armour-plate. Thus it is that the cannon-ball has, after so many years of use, disappeared from modern guns, and that its place is taken by an elongated projectile with a head in the form of a Gothic arch, and having a total length of some 3 to 3⅝ calibres.

The alteration of the form of the projectile, it will be seen, gives us the power of passing through the air to the object to be struck, without losing so much of the initial velocity as was lost by the old spherical form, and also the greater power of attack, per unit of area struck; but there are difficulties of a serious character attendant upon this change.

We have hitherto regarded the subject, from the point of view that a certain muzzle velocity existed, without considering how that muzzle velocity was produced ; but we must now enquire into the main duty of the gun, which is the production of the muzzle velocity.

From this point of view the change of form of the shot is a very grave matter. It is a matter involving no less, than the change from smooth-bore to rifle-bore, the change in the length of the gun, the change in the nature and in the quality of the powder, and eventually, as will appear, the change from muzzle loading to breech loading.

Let us now look into these questions. Obviously that which gives the velocity to the shot, must be the pressure of the powder, acting on the area of the base of the shot throughout its travel in the gun, and if there are two shots of equal weight and equal length of travel in the gun, it is clear that, whatever their form, or whatever the area of the bore of the gun, i. e. of the base of the shot, the total average pressure must be the same. Let us see how this operates in the cases we have before considered, that of a spherical projectile of 68 lbs. weight in an 8-inch gun, and that of a cylinder of 68 lbs. weight, but 15 inches long, in a 5-inch gun. The respective areas of these calibres are as 64 to 25; if therefore the total pressures are to be the same, the pressure per square inch must be increased from a mean of 25 in the case of the 8-inch gun, to a mean of 64 in the 5-inch gun. That is, to give a 5-inch diameter long projectile of 68 lbs. weight the same muzzle velocity as a 68 lbs. spherical projectile of 8-inch diameter, after traversing the same length of barrel, the mean pressure must be 2·72, or nearly 2¾ times as much.

Further, it will be found that in the 5-inch gun, the same weight of powder will no longer do the same work on the shot, as it would in the 8-inch.

A gun is, after all, only an engine, with its piston (the shot) moving at a very high velocity, and the powder gases act on the shot very much in the same way, in which steam acts upon the piston, in an expansive steam engine, after the admission from the boiler is shut off, and expansion has begun. We know that in these engines the useful effect of the steam increases, in a certain ratio, as the number of expansions increase. Now if, for example, a shot travel of, say 80 inches were given alike to the projectile of an 8-inch gun, and to that of the 5-inch gun, and an equal quantity of powder be used in each case, the powder occupying a cubic contents of, say 500 inches, the expansion in the instance of the 8-inch gun would be 9 times, while in the 5-inch gun it would be only 4½ times.

A remedy for this condition of things, is to be found in lengthening the barrel of the 5-inch gun, so as to give a greater travel, under pressure, to the shot. This operates bene-

ficially in two ways; the one that the shot is subjected to the
pressure for a longer period, and that therefore a less intensity
of pressure suffices; the other, that the number of expansions
are increased, and more duty is got out of the powder.

But it will be found that to give in the 5-inch gun the
low average pressure, and the number of expansions obtaining
in the 8-inch gun, in their entirety, a very undesirable piece of
artillery, would have to be made. Assume, as we have, that the
spherical shot of the 8-inch gun had a travel of 80 inches
or 10 calibres, the travel to be given to the 5-inch projectile
to obtain the conditions of pressure and of powder duty
obtaining in the 8-inch gun must be as much as 205
inches = to 41 calibres of that gun. Such means, therefore,
of obtaining the desired total pressure on the smaller area can
only be partially followed. The length cannot for practical
purposes be increased to anything like this extent, and therefore
a higher average pressure must prevail, involving the employ-
ment of more powder, and powder of a nature that will keep
up a sustained pressure; a continued shove, rather than a
blow.

We have seen, that in order to reduce the rate of diminution
of the muzzle velocity, and in order to concentrate the striking
energy, it is necessary to employ an elongated projectile, but
the use of such a projectile lands us in another difficulty,
requiring another remedy, accompanied of course by its own
attendant difficulties: the elongated projectile would, if fired
without rotation being imparted to it, very soon "turn over,"
as it is called, and would lose its true direction, were it not
given the spinning motion, obtained by rifling the gun.

This rifling involves wounding the bore of the gun, by
making in it a number of grooves, each one of which is an
invitation to the commencement of a crack, and it also involves
the absorption of part of the energy of the powder, in producing
the rotation of the projectile.

And with respect to this question, of the whole energy of the
powder not being spent in propelling the shot, I trust I may

be pardoned for a somewhat lengthy digression, to bring before your minds a circumstance which is so often overlooked.

It must not be supposed that the energy of the powder is all utilised in driving out the projectile, and in giving it rotation. On the contrary, a very considerable percentage is employed in moving the powder itself along the gun in the rear of the shot, while as regards the question of recoil, a large portion of this is due to the energy required to expel the whole of the powder gases, at the enormous velocity at which they are expelled, after the exit of the shot has left them free issue. One's feeling is that it cannot need much work to expel a mere gas, but you may depend upon it that if 700 lbs. of powder are put into a gun in the solid state—in which condition you would agree they could not be expelled from the gun, with less absorption of energy than would be needed to expel a shot of the same weight, issuing at the same velocity—the fact of having converted this 700 lbs. of solid into gas, will not make it weigh less, and thus, as I have said, a considerable proportion of the energy will have to be expended, to move the gases along the bore in the rear of the shot, fortunately, at a mean velocity much less than that of the shot. As tested by the recoil, however, a much larger proportion of the energy will be found to be expended in causing the vehement rush of powder gas, after the shot has left the gun. About the effects of powder gas I shall have something to say further on.

We have now traced the change from the smooth-bore gun firing a spherical shot, to a rifled gun firing an elongated projectile ; needing heavier total pressure per inch of surface to propel it ; pressure to be obtained, partly by increasing the weight of the charge (involving a greater length of powder-chamber), and partly by increasing the length of the gun for the travel of the shot, both alterations demanding the production of a much longer weapon.

The question now arises, How are these longer guns to be loaded ?

Breech-loading presents, as I will show you later on, enormous difficulties. Let us therefore endeavour to adhere to the simple muzzle loading. Very well. Let us see, however, whether in a ship this is practicable. Take the 13½-inch gun, with only 25½ calibres of length, to include powder-chamber and all—a comparatively short gun. To sponge it out there must be some 30 feet of rammer. Obviously, if the gun were to be used as a broadside gun, it would need to be run in, until its breech would be touching the opposite side of even a wide ship. Well, what is to be done? Put the gun in a central turret, and load fore and aft? Yes, but where? the gun must fire over the upper deck : are the men to be on the upper deck exposed to the full fire of the enemy, while the ship and the turret are both armoured? That won't do. What is the remedy? Why, have two ports in the turret for each gun, one on the level above the upper deck for firing, the other on a level below that deck for loading, by depressing the muzzle of the gun. Well, having done this, and having resolved to face the difficulty of shoving the charge, up the inclined bore of a depressed gun, down which the charge is always tending to return—a tendency that may be aggravated by the rolling motion of the ship, and that must be resisted by the use of wads—even then there is not space for a full-length rammer, and further, the power of the men to force the enormous weight of projectile up the inclined bore is insufficient. What must be done ? Why, make an hydraulic telescopic rammer, thus economising space and obtaining the desired power, while affording the protection of the armour to the men. Yes, with the possibility of not knowing how far the telescopic rammer is really projected (for it is invisible, being inside the gun), and that thus there may be placed on a charge which has failed to ignite, another charge, and that then the gun, being double loaded, may go off the next time and burst, as on one occasion really happened.

But there are other objections to the muzzle loading of rifled guns. The shot must have such an amount of clearance (" windage " over its body and over its projections which are to fit into the rifling) as will admit of its being readily introduced, and not sticking fast in the operation. Through this clearance the powder gases will rush, and will rapidly erode the surface of the bore. Something must be provided to prevent this. Something was provided, called a gas-check. This consisted of a disc of copper attached to the base of the projectile, and of such diameter that it could be passed down the bore from the muzzle, but so constructed, that on firing, the pressure of the powder gases should swell it out, and cause it to fill up the bore and the rifle grooves themselves.

This may be the right time to give you an instance of the power of powder gases in eroding steel.

I have here a steel cylinder 5½ inches long, and having through its axis a cylindrical hole of a little over a fifth of an inch in diameter. This cylinder is to be screwed into a vessel containing 13 lbs. of powder, and the hole forms the only outlet from the vessel. On the powder being fired, the whole 13 lbs. of gases rush out through this hole, with the result shown by a corresponding cylinder, which has been used in an experiment. This result is, that the hole which was, before the firing, so small as only to admit a pen-holder, is now by the one passage of the gases of 13 lbs. of powder increased to such a diameter as to admit my forefinger.

When tested by weighing, it will be found that with the quality of steel of which this sample was composed, nearly ¾ lb. of steel has been removed.

This instance will give some idea of the effect in the bore of a gun, of a rush of gas past the projectile.

A further objection to muzzle-loading was this, that although the gas-check might thoroughly fit the bore when it was expanded, it did not steady the projectile as a driving band does, and thus the extreme accuracy of the shooting was impaired.

The remedy for all this is no doubt breech loading. With breech-loading guns the length of barrel may be indefinitely increased without adding to the difficulty of inserting the charge; the cartridge not having to pass down the bore may have any reasonable increase of diameter. Moreover, in lieu of a gas-check, and in lieu of studs taking into the rifling, the projectile can be fitted with a driving band made larger than the bore of the gun, which being forced by the powder pressure on the first movement of the shot into the rifle grooves, fills them up, and prevents the passage of gas. Further, the rifle grooves themselves, instead of being few in number and large to receive studs, are made many in number and of but little depth, and thereby the barrel is not so deeply wounded and the projectile is steadied in the bore more accurately; better shooting can be obtained, wads are of course dispensed with, and all chance of double loading is of necessity at an end.

But let us see what demands are made on the gun constructor, by the provision of breech loading, to fulfil these ends.

The breech opening, to be really efficacious, must be of such diameter as to admit of a powder charge having all but the diameter of the powder chamber, that is to say, that in a 12-inch gun the diameter of the breech opening is not less than 16 inches, and in the 110-ton gun is as much as 21 inches.

The pressure although only intended to be some 17 tons on the inch, must, as a measure of precaution, be estimated as considerably in excess of this; but take this 17 tons per inch; in the 12-inch gun, it will give us a total strain of 3400 tons, and in the case of the 110-ton gun a strain of as much as 5800 tons. I will ask those practical men who are here, to remember, how, if for any purpose we desired to fit a vessel, that is to bear some two or three tons per inch water pressure, with a 20-inch cover, we should provide numerous massive bolts and nuts, how we should screw them down one after another, and with what pains we should endeavour to make the joint, and the length of time that would be consumed, even when working at our best, and undisturbed by the attack of an enemy. I will ask that this may be borne in mind, while considering how great must be the difficulties that attend upon making the joint of the breech of even a 12-inch gun, in but a few seconds of time, to resist 3400 tons of pressure, and to be absolutely gas-tight.

I have shown you what the simple passage of the gas of but 13 lbs. of powder can do in the way of erosion, and I will ask you to consider the result of a gas-leak, when there are hundreds of pounds of powder seeking escape.

Moreover, this joint has not only to be rapidly made, and to be absolutely tight, but when the gun has been fired the joint has to be as rapidly unmade; it must be a joint, therefore, that even under the enormous pressure, has not swelled out so as to stick fast, and thus prevent the ready opening of the breech.

These, I think it will be agreed, are no light problems, and yet they have to be solved before a working breech closure is obtained.

We will now consider the structure of the gun. It may be said, why not select the metal—cast iron, bronze, or steel—and having determined on the pressure to be resisted, and the factor of safety to be allowed, and knowing the resisting power of the metal you have selected, make the walls thick enough, and then all that is needed has been attended to. Happy would it be for the gun-maker, if a gun could be produced of reasonable strength, combined with manageable weight, by such simple means; but the following consideration will show that this construction is not one suited for Big Guns.

Assume that I have, interposed between my hand, and a pound weight I desire to lift, a spiral spring, say 1 foot long, and of such a character that it must extend 1 inch before it can raise the weight; and assume that I have another spiral spring, precisely similar to the first one, except the length, which is to be 2 feet: it is clear that if I employ this second spring to raise a pound weight it must extend 2 inches before it would do this. In other words, the percentage of extension must be equal. Now, suppose that one has a gun, of say 1 foot bore, with the walls 6 inches thick, making the external diameter 2 feet: it is obvious that, in order for the imaginary circle of metal at the outside of this two feet to be as effective in resisting the powder pressure as is the imaginary circle of metal of 1 foot diameter close to the bore, the increase of diameter of that outer circle should be twice that

of the increase of the diameter of the circle at the bore; for if
not, the percentage of extension would not be equal. But so
far from this being the case, it will be found (assuming the
density of the metal to remain unaltered) that when the gun
expands under firing, the actual extension of the imaginary
circle at the outside of the gun, will be only one-half of that of
the imaginary circle at the bore, and its percentage of extension
therefore will only be one-quarter; in other words, the percentage
of extension, and therefore the power to resist, decreases, as the
square of the distance from the centre of the gun, measured in
radii of the bore, increases.

Reverting to the two spiral springs, it is as though you were
told to employ the 1-foot and the 2-foot spring together for the
lifting of the weight, but with the injunction that whenever
you stretched the 1-foot spring a length of "one," you should
stretch the 2-foot spring a length of "a half" only—being one-
fourth the percentage of extension. If this were done, and the
two springs were employed to lift a weight of 1¼ lbs., it would
be found that the 1-foot spring was doing one pound of the work
while the 2-foot spring was doing only a quarter of a pound.

Let us assume that the designer of the supposed gun of 1-foot
bore, with sides 6 inches thick, was of opinion it was not
sufficiently strong, and that he determined to add to that
strength by doubling the thickness of the walls: these being
now 1 foot thick, the outside diameter of the gun would be
3 feet; but from what I have told you, you will be prepared
to hear that the value of the imaginary circle of metal at the
outside of this three feet diameter, is only one-ninth of the
value of the imaginary circle of metal at the bore. The result
would be, that while with the gun of 2 feet diameter, the
sectional area of the metal, and therefore its weight, would be
represented by $2^2 - 1^2 = 3$, the sectional area, and therefore
the weight, of the thickened gun would be represented by
$3^2 - 1^2 = 8$; while it would be found, from the reasons before
stated, that this increase of weight from 3 to 8 or 2⅔ times,
would only add ⅓rd to the former resisting power; and this is

always assuming that no practical difficulties arose in the pouring of so ponderous a casting and none from contraction in the cooling, that is to say, assuming the 12-inch thick casting were as trustworthy as the 6-inch thick.

It can readily be understood from a consideration of the foregoing, how it may be possible to extend, under the strain of firing, the skin of the bore, to a point where rupture will begin, while the metal towards the exterior should be so little elongated that it afforded no sufficient aid to this skin.

It is with the view of curing these defects, that the system of putting an initial compressive strain on the inner metal, by means of an initial tensile strain on the outer metal, has been devised and adopted. By this system it is possible to much more justly distribute the strain, and to greatly reduce that on the immediate wall of the bore.

Attempts have been made to obtain this external initial compression, in large cast-iron guns, by casting them hollow, on a metal core, and by passing, as soon as the casting had been made, streams of water through the centre, with the object of compelling the outside when it cooled down, to set in a state of tension upon an already solidified centre. A considerable number of guns were made, in the United States, on this construction, but the results were not trustworthy, as many of them broke up spontaneously from the effect of the internal strains.

The attempt to obtain the desired result, by such treatment of the metal of a casting while cooling, has, for the present at all events, been given up, and the system of shrinking on hoops is pursued.

To fulfil the condition of obtaining the very best effect from the metal, the hoops should be very numerous and very thin; but in this, as in many cases, it is better to sacrifice a small percentage of effect, to obtain simplicity of manufacture, and thus in a gun built up of turned and bored hoops, it is found on the whole desirable, to make these of such dimensions, that from two to five thicknesses of hoops, depending on the size of the gun, are employed.

But there is another construction of gun, which admits of the theoretical calculations being much more nearly followed. I allude to the system of coiling flat steel wire, or ribbon, around the tube, laying on these coils cold, and under predetermined tensions. There are many hopeful features about this system.

Steel in the form of wire, or ribbon, is in a condition of very great tensile strength. The section of the material being so small, it is very unlikely there can be any concealed flaws. Moreover, if there are any, it is very unlikely that in the successive layers of ribbon, such flaws would be aggregated in the same part of the winding, and thus there is hardly any chance of a considerable local weakness. Further, if there be a flaw it cannot go on spreading, as it may do through solid metal, but must be confined to its own layer. These are all-important elements in favour of the use of steel wire or ribbon, and I believe if we had simply to consider the question of fortifying a cylinder, to resist circumferential strain and nothing else, wire might unhesitatingly be adopted. In these days of machine guns, and of quick-firing guns, however, there is always a chance that a " Big Gun " may be struck by one of their bullets, and it might well be that a bullet, which was too small to inflict serious injury upon a gun reinforced by solid steel hoops, would cut the wire coils to pieces, and would thus temporarily render the Big Gun unserviceable. This chance renders it necessary to enclose the wire, in some kind of jacket, that shall be sufficient to afford protection against bullets from such artillery. Moreover, in a breech-loading gun, the question of longitudinal strength, and the due connection with the trunnions has to be taken into account, and hence further difficulties arise with the wire construction. These difficulties have, however, in a great measure, been already successfully grappled with in England, and there are now some four or five guns and howitzers under experiment, the largest being a gun of $10\frac{1}{4}$ inches bore, having a length of about 29 calibres.

So far the results have been promising, at least in England. The French have found the means they provided for giving longitudinal strength were not satisfactory, and I am not aware that they are continuing their experiments. In the United States a wire gun was made, and it was sought to give the required endway strength, by immersing the gun in a bath of brazing metal, to braze all the wire coils together. The first attempt was unsatisfactory, and it appears to me to be one in the wrong direction. I believe, but am not certain, the subject of wire guns is still under consideration in the United States.

Unsatisfactory as the result of wire gun construction has been in France, and in the United States, we are still pursuing the subject, and I trust the time is not far distant when guns on this construction will be in the service.

In the meantime we cannot afford to be without guns, and we must manufacture guns, such as artillerists all over the world agree, should be employed. The construction of these guns is one where the central tube is reinforced, in part or in whole, depending on the size of the gun, with hoops shrunk on, the guns being breech-loading, and rifled.

And now as regards the great increase in the size of the guns which has taken place within the last few years. How has it arisen? The answer is, from the struggle between the guns and the armour plates—the Attack and the Defence.

Twenty-five years ago the armour plate of the *Warrior* was of wrought iron and was 4½ inches thick.

Feeble as we now think such armour, it was sufficient to resist cast-iron spherical shot. These impinged upon it and indented it, but the shot broke up into a sort of conical nail with its head against the plate, while the rest of the ball was wedged to pieces as it were by the cone formed out of its own vitals, and spread in fragments laterally over the face of the plate. It became evident that some different form of projectile, and some other material were needed.

I have already pointed out to you how the elongated projectile, concentrates the energy of the shot on the surface attacked, but it will be clear that this effect must be reciprocal, and that the energy will be, in like manner, concentrated on the projectile itself, and that therefore some material far better than mere ordinary cast iron, must be resorted to; and you will be prepared to hear that steel was selected, even in those early days, when steel manufacture was still in a very backward condition. The difficulty, however, of producing proper projectiles was great; they were either too soft or too hard; they often spent their energy in deforming themselves in the one case, or, in the other case, they broke into pieces on the plate, if indeed they had not failed in the act of hardening and tempering.

Then came the proposition of chilled cast-iron projectiles. I believe that any one who had had experience with chilled metal, would have been disposed to say, " Of all materials this one is " the most unlikely, for it is as brittle as the highest tempered " steel." This may be true, but it possessed a hardness such as enabled its point to support the vast pressure brought on it by the concentrated energy, without being deformed and blunted, and to bury itself in the iron plate. When once this burying in of the point is effected, a very curious result follows. The brittle shot is bound together by the very plate it is penetrating, and in this manner perforates it, without change of form, although the structure of the shot is so far destroyed, that if the plate were thin enough to allow the shot to pass through, and it struck a second plate behind the first, it would flow away on the surface of this second plate, as the original cast-iron ball, would have flowed over the surface of the first plate.

An analogous instance, is to be found in the impression that may be made in a leaden surface by a sealing-wax seal when laid upon it, and struck a powerful blow; the brittle wax impresses the lead, being held together from dispersion by the lead itself, although in the act of impression the seal is disintegrated.

That the chilled projectile spent its energy in perforating the armour-plate, and not in self-deformation, was clearly proved by the fact, that the fragments from the interior of a chilled projectile were, immediately after impact, cold to the touch, while those of steel projectiles were extremely hot, and could not be handled.

Thanks to the chilled projectile, the gun was master of the wrought-iron armour plates, of the thickness then made; upon which the Defence said, " We must make the plates thicker and " keep out the shot," and they did so. Then the Attack said, " I must make my guns bigger," and they did so; and thus the increase went on. The guns seemed to be getting the best of it, for armour plate had reached a thickness which it appeared impossible to increase, if the vessel were to have any carrying power left for guns and coals, when the Defence hit upon a new expedient. Instead of making the plate entirely of wrought iron, they composed it of about two-thirds wrought iron at the back, united metallically to one-third of steel for the face· Hardness in front, and toughness behind. In this way it was found that, speaking roundly, a 12-inch compound plate was able to do the duty of an 18-inch wrought-iron plate; and further than this, the compound plate proved more than a match for chilled projectiles; they could not effectively enter the hard face so as to be supported by the metal they were penetrating, and were broken up. The effort was then made to master the plates by still further increasing the bore of the guns, making the shot of such prodigious size (over 2000 lbs. in weight) as to conquer the plate by smashing it, rather than by penetrating it. Time will not admit of my going into the subject of the efforts that are being made, and with great prospect of success, to manufacture steel projectiles which shall successfully contend with hard-faced or compound armour.

It is, as I have said, from the continued efforts of the Attack and of the Defence that the dimensions of our Big Guns have gone on increasing and increasing, until their weight has reached 110 tons, their length 44 feet, the weight of their projectile 1800 lbs., and that of their powder-charge 820 lbs. So that the *Benbow*, one of our last new ironclads, with 10,000 tons displacement, has for her powerful armament only two such guns, being provided, however, with ten 6-inch broadside guns;

while the "three-decker" the *Duke of Wellington*, whose screw-propeller trials I well remember taking place when I was engaged in conducting other screw-propeller trials at Portsmouth, in the year 1853, a vessel of only 6070 tons displacement, had an armament of 131 guns, the largest of which, however, was, I believe, only a 32-pounder, and, if so, weighed no more than 56 cwt.

Now we have shown, that in order to obtain good duty out of the metal employed, the outer metal of the gun must be subjected to an initial tensile strain, and that, pending the solution of the wire gun question, that strain must be given by hooping. The question next arises, what metal shall we use? I leave out of consideration, for our purposes of to-night, various metals that are from time to time proposed, because they are still in the experimental stage, and the duty of those charged with providing the nation with its means of defence, is to employ for service, only those materials, and those systems of construction, which have passed that stage.

Under this condition of things the gun-constructor finds himself called on to select from cast iron, from wrought iron, and from steel. Having regard to the work which the rifling has to perform, and to other considerations, steel is clearly the metal that one would desire to employ for the central tube. As regards the hoops, one would not be inclined to suggest cast iron, and there remain, therefore, only wrought iron and steel. For a considerable period wrought iron was used for this purpose, and very well it did its work; made as a very long bar, and coiled into a helix of the desired dimensions, the successive convolutions were welded together at one operation, and in this manner the desired cylinder, or jacket was forged, having the grain of the iron running round about it in the best direction, for acting as a circumferential reinforcement to the tube.

But some few years since, after much investigation and after consultation with steel manufacturers, it was determined to use this material for all parts of the gun.

I must now ask your attention for a short time to the subject of steel.

And first, what is steel? How was it made and manipulated a few years since? How is it made now?

As to what it is, I suppose the text-book would tell us that it is the element iron united to a small proportion of the element carbon, and is a material which in these respects lies between wrought iron and cast iron. In practice, no doubt, there are commonly other constituents, such as manganese, for example, but for the purposes of to-night it will suffice that we look upon steel as being composed of iron and of carbon.

It is not so many years since, that steel was made by the cementation process, that is by heating bars of wrought iron in contact with charcoal, until they had become sufficiently carbonised. These bars were, from the appearance of their surface, known as blister steel; they might either be worked from their then condition, or they might be broken into fragments, selected for degree of carbonisation, then be put into a crucible and melted to produce cast steel. Each crucible contained but a few pounds weight, and the resulting ingot, cast in a metal mould, was rarely heavier than the charge of one crucible, although occasionally the contents of more than one crucible were used, to make an exceptionally large ingot. The ingot having been drawn out, the result was the cast-steel bar used for cutlery and for engineers' chisels and turning tools, a material that was produced in quantities stated in pounds, and that was sold at so much a pound, and was an article of luxury.

I do not wish to be trapped into repeating to you to-night my lecture of 1877 on the Future of Steel, and I will therefore pass over the attempts to make steel by the puddling process, by the Chenot process, and by the Uchatius process; neither will I say anything about that important branch of industry, steel casting, but I will come at once to the three modes by which in these days, ingots for large forgings are produced.

The crucible plan (the oldest mode, and one which still survives, although I believe it is rapidly dying out) is to employ as many hundreds of crucibles as the size of the ingot needs, to have their contents ready, and to pour them in succession into the ingot mould.

Another way is to make the steel by the converter plan, wherein fused cast iron is decarbonised, by the blowing in of air, which burns off the carbon, leaving the contents of the vessel in the state of fluid wrought iron, and then to run in so much of a metal rich in carbon as shall give to the whole charge, the proportion required. The third mode, the open hearth, consists in melting the material in gas furnaces, and so proportioning the mixture, as to obtain the desired amount of carbonisation, ascertaining before tapping, what the condition really is, by means of test pieces.

For gun purposes, we may confine our attention to the first, and to the third of these three modes. The ingot is, in either case, cast vertically, and in order to obtain freedom from blow-holes and other imperfections, the upper part is cut off and is rejected. Commonly, if the weight of the forging is to be 30 tons, the ingot as cast may be from 45 to 50 tons, that is, only some 60 per cent. are used, while some 40 per cent. are rejected.

Now I need hardly say, that ingots of 50 tons, are a considerable time in solidifying, and during this time an effect takes place, which is a source of trouble, and of uncertainty. The carbon tends to separate out, and to come upwards, with the result, that even if the whole mass had when run, a perfectly uniform percentage of carbon throughout, by the time a large ingot has set, there will be found a decrease of carbon at the lower end, and an increase of carbon at the upper end. You must not think this a matter of slight importance, for assuming all other things to be equal, it may be said, roughly speaking, that unless in every thousand parts of the steel, there are present about two and a half parts of carbon, the metal will be too "low" or "mild," while if there be more than about four parts, the metal will be too "high" for the purposes of gun manufacture.

Allowance has to be made, therefore, in proportioning the

carbon in the original mass, so that after this separating out of the carbon, in the solidifying of the ingot, enough shall remain in the lower part, and too much shall not be found in the upper part, of that portion of the ingot which is used.

After casting the ingot has to be forged.

Now as regards the question of forging, men of my age, when we were boys, did not know of a steam hammer; our knowledge of heavy hammers was confined to double-hand hammers and to helves.

At length the steam hammer in various forms was everywhere to be met with, and it appeared, that in it we possessed, an implement, competent to deal with any such mass of wrought iron, as the arts would ever need. But now forgings of previously unheard-of dimensions, and forgings not of comparatively plastic iron, but of steel, are required. I will ask you to think what is needed in the forging of a mass, say with the object of diminishing its diameter and of adding to its length; is it not clear that the blow in order to be efficacious should make itself felt to the very core of the piece under treatment? Common sense tells us that one might hammer in perpetuity with a carpenter's hammer upon an iron shaft, of comparatively small diameter, with the result, indeed, of bruising and injuring the mere surface, but with no effect upon the centre of the mass.

Similarly, with even large steam hammers, they may, while doing their work of elongation on a large forging, have an injurious effect, by tending to extend the exterior layers more speedily, than the interior can readily follow, and thus there may be set up in the very act of manufacture, injurious internal strains.

To avoid this danger there are now being introduced machines which forge, not by percussion, as hammers do, but by steady pressure.

Assume the forging to be made; it has to be bored, it has to be turned, and then it has to be "oil-hardened," a process requiring special plant, and uncommon care that strains are not set up in the very process which is intended to improve the quality. Annealing is carried out with the object of mitigating strains if they exist, but with the danger, that you may, if not very careful, undo, or partially undo in the annealing, the benefits arising from oil-hardening.

You will no doubt expect to hear that the tube is tested, and this is so, as far and as well as circumstances will permit. A gun forging is not like a cheese, you can't put the "taster" in where you will and as frequently as you will; for this obviously would ruin the forging for the purpose for which it is intended. Such testing would be open to the objection that used to be made when it was suggested a needle should be tested, which was, "It can't be done, for if it bends it is no good; if it breaks "it is good; but you have destroyed your needle in ascertaining its goodness." There are only two places from which you can afford to take test specimens of a gun-tube, and these are from the two ends—the breech end and the muzzle end. From these places, by making the tube longer than is needed for the gun, specimens can be taken. A set of conditions to be fulfilled by these test pieces, was drawn up after much thought; among these tests were comprised those for extension, for ultimate strength, neither too "high" nor too "low," and for the power of bending over a certain size semicircular presser, under a steady pressure. The large steel manufacturers who were in a condition as regards "plant" to make the heavy forgings needed (with one exception) said, "We have made the forgings, they "will not pass the tests; it is not the forgings which are in "fault, but the tests which are too high, these must be relaxed." Gun manufacture was in danger of being altogether stopped.

Evidence was taken from the manufacturers, and it was found they were not unanimous in the nature of the alterations they desired. One man was content with test A, but held test B in abhorrence, while another had no objection to B if he could but be relieved of A. After conference, it was determined that in the then state of the manufacture, the tests should in certain points be relaxed, and greater ranges of elastic limit and of ultimate strength were admitted. I am glad to say, as time has gone on, steel manufacture has improved, and improved tests are complied with.

Having tested the two ends of the tube, and found that its breech end is not too " low " and its muzzle end not too " high," one is entitled to hope that the steel situated between these two limits will not be " lower " than the one, nor " higher " than the other but will bear such relation to the end tests, as its position between breech and muzzle would lead one to anticipate. And I believe that if the steel has been made by the open hearth process, this hope will not be a vain one, and I also believe that it may be justified in many cases where the crucible process is employed.

With respect to this latter process, I should say, there are certain foreign Governments who still insist on its being followed; indeed the French Government, for the special case of certain small parts, make its use, or made its use in 1882, when their tests were drawn up, obligatory.

But I have known a quite recent case, of the failure of the tube of a large cannon—one of those I shall have to allude to hereafter--where within a very short distance, the carbon varied very nearly in the proportion of from one to two. This tube was made by the crucible process.

Assume, however, that the tube has been made by the open hearth process, and that this does secure regularity of composition, within the limits shown by the end test pieces. there still remains, and must always, I fear, remain, the risk of internal flaws in the casting.

You may test the quality, you may follow a process which may, and probably will, give uniformity of quality within certain limits, but you never can be sure there may not be a latent defect; and a defect that no subsequent process can completely cure, for remember, that steel must be forged at a temperature considerably below the welding point, and that thus, although the act of forging may press the walls of this hidden cavity together, that act can never make sound metallic connection between them.

In forging wrought iron at a welding heat, you may, if there be no foreign substance interposed, weld together soundly the sides of a cavity, but you cannot effect this in forging steel. Do not, however, suppose I am desirous of introducing welding processes; far from it. In fact, between wrought iron and steel you are in this dilemma. In wrought iron every weld is a matter of uncertainty, and in making a steel ingot you never can be sure there may not exist some latent flaw.

That this is no imaginary case the following instance will show. A 6-inch gun (to which I shall also allude hereafter), one of the second kind that were made, and therefore technically known as a Mark 2 gun, after having fired 278 rounds, burst, and it was found that in the front part of the powder-chamber there was a flaw, the two sides of which had been forged close together, but had never been in metallic union; this cell lay embedded in the thickness of the wall of the chamber, and the boring tool had just not broken into it, there was a thin skin of sound metal left. The erosion, however, had at last worn a way into this flattened cell—a mere crack, for its sides were so close together—the powder gases entered, and pressing on the sides of the cell-crack, gradually spread it, as a wedge might have done, along that which had previously been solid metal, until the flaw was so far increased that the next round caused the burst. The marks of the internal extension, that had been going on, were very obvious after the explosion, and were very interesting as telling the history of that which resulted in the burst.

It would be a great boon indeed to all engaged in metallurgical operations, if the electrician could succeed in indicating the existence of latent flaws.

Experiments are being carried out now, to see whether it is possible, to try the whole tube (before it is built up into the gun), by internal shock pressure tests, and I think that these experiments may result in success; but if they do they will after all not be absolutely conclusive, any more than the proof of the finished gun is conclusive. I have but little doubt, if a shock test had been applied to the 6-inch gun to which I have alluded, that, so long as the entrance to the cell was covered by the sound skin, the tube would not have failed under the test, even although it would not have had the external reinforcement, as it had when it burst.

I have called your attention to some of the difficulties attendant upon the successful manufacture of a Big Gun, to attain the desired end of powerful and good shooting. I wish time admitted of my speaking to you on the subject of the difficulties of judging the pressure prevailing in different localities in the gun, how that it can only be done by so filling the gun with gauges, or with wires for the chronoscope as to render it useless for service; or, if probably the best mode of all be used, by actually cutting the gun to pieces, taking off successive lengths, and recording the corresponding muzzle velocities of the projectile.

I wish I could have spoken, as I had intended, on the subject of wave pressure, and of the results arising from it, and that I could have gone into the question connected with this and with the other important subject, the sustaining a considerable pressure along the bore of the gun, including the nature of the powder; that I could have spoken to you about the mode, and the place of the ignition of the powder, of the means that are employed for this end, and of the precautions taken. Further, I should have been glad to say something about shells and their fuzes, and something about gun carriages; about the means for dealing with recoil, and the means of working big guns. Time will not admit of any of this being done, and I must occupy that which remains with other matters relating to the gun question—matters that, as members of a nation that wishes to be able to defend itself from the covetousness of other nations, you feel, and justly feel, are of vital importance.

You are probably saying to yourselves, we see frequent statements from persons, whom we presume to be of repute, that no proper progress is made in English guns; that they are behind those of other nations; that they are less trust-

worthy than those of other nations; that one hears of failure,
after failure; that one hears of the guns rapidly wearing out,
even if they do not give way; and that one does not hear of
these things in the case of foreign guns. Further, it is made a
matter of complaint that if there be some mode of construction
better than another, our guns are not all made in accordance
with that mode, but that they vary, and that some are inferior.

Let us see how the facts are. In 1874, the 12-inch 38-ton
muzzle-loading rifled gun, having a shot travel of 14 calibres,
composed of a steel tube with wrought iron coils around part
of it, was the foremost piece of ordnance we possessed. The
projectile of this gun weighed 700 lbs., its extreme length was
3 calibres, its velocity on leaving the muzzle was 1410 feet
per second, and its muzzle energy was 9650 foot-tons.

Let us take our present gun of the same calibre. It is
12 inches bore; weighs 45 tons; is breech-loading; is rifled
with multiple grooves, taking a rotating ring and not a gas-
check; it is made entirely of steel, and has a shot travel of
21½th calibres. The projectile of this gun weighs 714 lbs.; it
has an extreme length of 3 calibres; its velocity on leaving
the muzzle is 1900 feet per second; and its muzzle energy is
18,000 foot-tons.

You will see that in these few years we have converted a
muzzle velocity of 1410 into one of 1900, and have done so
with the same projectile, and that we have all but doubled the
muzzle energy, although the addition to the weight of the gun
does not amount to more than 20 per cent.

I call this progress, and very good progress.

Again, as regards dimensions of weapons: whereas in 1874
the 38-ton muzzle-loader was the largest gun we had ever
made, we are now making 110-ton guns, entirely of steel and
breech-loading, having a shot travel of 25 calibres, a weight of
projectile of 1800 lbs., a muzzle velocity of 2100 feet per second,
and a muzzle energy of 55,040 foot-tons.

I call that substantial progress.

With respect to progress in construction, I may remind you

that we are continuing our experiments with steel ribbon guns.

You may, however, say, " It does not suffice to have our present " guns, compared with our former guns, although no doubt that " is one test of progress; they should be compared with the pre- " sent guns of other nations."

Well, let us do so, with the guns of say, France, Germany, and Italy. The United States I will not refer to, as I cannot believe that any unwisdom of our respective rulers would be allowed to place in collision, peoples speaking the same language, of the same race, and having so much in common.

The facts as regards France, so far as I know them, are that their largest steel guns are of 75 tons weight, and of 16½ inches bore, firing a projectile weighing 1720 lbs., with a muzzle velocity of 1739 feet per second, giving an energy of 36,000 foot-tons. The gun is breech-loading, and is rifled on the increasing twist system, as the English guns are. It is true the French possess a 96-ton gun, but this is largely composed of cast iron, and has only the same bore and ballistics, as the 75-ton steel gun before mentioned.

As regards Germany, I do not believe that the Germans have in their service any guns larger than (if indeed they be so large as) the steel guns I have mentioned as belonging to France, although no doubt the great German gun-maker is prepared to manufacture for them, as he has done for the Italians, guns up to 119 tons.

The facts as regards Italy are that, except two 119-ton guns just referred to, her other Big Guns of 100 and 105 tons have been manufactured in this country. With respect to the 119-ton guns, I am informed their ballistics are as follows:— weight of charge, 727 lbs.; weight of shot, 2314 lbs.; muzzle velocity, 1772 feet per second, and muzzle energy, 50,324 foot-tons.

It may be interesting to compare the ballistics of the 105-ton guns, which are:—weight of charge, 900 lbs.; weight of shot, 2000 lbs.; muzzle velocity, 2019 feet per second, and muzzle energy, 56,547 foot-tons.

I think you will agree I am justified in saying that the position of **Italy** as regards Big Guns is no more than on a par with our own.

Now I think, the foregoing statements should satisfy you we are not lagging behind other nations, but are well to the front, while, as I have said, with regard to wire-gun experiments, I believe we have done, and are doing, more than has been attempted by any other nation.

You may say, this is all very well, you have shown us that you make guns equal in power to those of other nations, but we are told that your guns when made, are worse than those of other nations, that they fail, and that those of other nations do not fail.

Well, let us see what the extent of our failure is. This we do know; what the failure of foreign nations may be, we do not know with certainty, as they (as far as possible) keep their failures to themselves.

I presume you will be satisfied, if, under the title of " Big Guns," we confine our attention to breech-loading guns of 6 inches bore—a size of about one-third of the weight of the 8-inch gun in the Inventions Exhibition—and those exceeding 6-inch bore, and if we go back say some six years.

We have in the service, or are making up to this time, in all some three hundred or four hundred 6-inch guns. These have been made in successive lots, and on each occasion such improvements have been introduced as experience has dictated, so that there are as many as five Marks, or stages of development, of these 6-inch guns.

From those already in the service, thousands of rounds have been fired, including the proof rounds and a considerable proportion of other rounds with full charges. As regards numbers of rounds per gun, I may cite cases of those guns which are used for drill and practice, where 1400 rounds have been fired.

With the exception of those of one of the Marks, these guns were not hooped in front of the trunnions. You may say, why were they not ? The answer is, that having regard to the calculated pressures, the guns were strong enough without, and that they are so, where there is no latent defect, is shown by the number of rounds that the unhooped classes have fired successfully. There are many temptations on the score of economy, and of simplicity, to adopt for the chase the unhooped mode of manufacture, for the 6-inch and for larger natures of guns, as is evidenced by its having been followed by every nation.

In addition to the 6-inch guns in the British service, or making for that service, there have been constructed by private manufacturers for foreign States, some hundreds of 6-inch guns of practically the same designs, and these guns have given satisfaction.

I will not give you a list of all our 8-inch, 9·2 inch, 12-inch, 13·5 inch, and 110-ton guns, but we have these guns in considerable numbers. Well, what has been the result, and what have been the bursts? Of guns issued to the service, two 6-inch and one 12-inch have failed. One of the 6-inch guns I have already alluded to when describing the effect of a concealed cavity; the second gun blew its unhooped chase off with a half-charge; and the 12-inch gun which I have also previously alluded to, blew its unhooped chase off with a three-quarter charge. In addition to these failures in service, there have been during experiment, and when the men were firing under special precautions, failures in two 9·2 inch 18-ton guns. All these five guns that have failed were unhooped at the chase, and were not steel guns, but were all of the early designs, composed of wrought iron and steel; and, as I have said, two of them burst with diminished charges. As regards the question of bursting with diminished charges, how does this strike you? As a circumstance to make the failure all the worse, or as a circumstance tending to show that the guns have not failed from faulty design? I have already stated that the 6-inch guns of all Marks have fired thousands of charges, many of which were full charges; it is clear, therefore, that the design is sufficient for a full charge, and à fortiori it must be for a half-charge; if therefore failure has taken place with half-charges, it is an evidence that it has arisen from some of those occult causes, which I have pointed out to you as existing to mar the success of the best designs—irregularity in the steel, concealed flaws, or internal strains. Paradox as it is, I would rather, when a particular nature or Mark of gun has stood full charges frequently, and without distress, that if one of these guns is to burst, it should do so with a half charge than with a full one.

Now for some of the failures of foreign guns.

It is now known that in May of last year, one of the French 75-ton 16½-inch steel guns blew its muzzle off, after it had satisfactorily passed the proof charges, and when firing a re-duced charge; the portion blown off was unhooped. A fellow gun was then examined, and was found to be cracked in the same part. Both guns have had the damaged parts removed, and have been re-issued in the shortened condition. I believe, it has been determined, that the remainder of the guns of this description shall be hooped to the muzzle.

In 1880, a 12½-inch gun failed at the third round. About these three failures I have no doubt. In addition to these, I have good reason to believe, but am not certain, that a 9½-inch steel gun burst in the chamber; the breech went one way, the muzzle the other, and the surrounding hoops dropped down into the gun-carriage; and also that a 6-inch steel gun blew off its unhooped muzzle.

These five instances all occurred with French guns.

As regards guns of German manufacture:—In 1877, at Con-stantinople, an 11-inch gun of 28 tons blew off the muzzle of an unhooped chase. From the *Weser Zeitung* it appears that in 1882, at Wilhelmshaven, a similar gun burst immediately in front of the last hoop on the chase; and from a letter in the *Times* in August 1879, it also appears that a 9½-inch gun, on board a German training frigate, burst into three pieces.

With respect to the United States: I cannot speak as to modern events, but I may say, it appears from a report of a Committee of the Senate in 1869, that in the eight preceding years there had been, in their cast-iron ordnance, varying in size from 15 inches smooth bore, down to 13-pounders, as many as 150 instances of guns bursting while being fired; while, as I have already mentioned, there were instances of spontaneous bursts, in 10 guns.

Last Tuesday evening's papers contained the report of the bursting of a gun at Genoa. I believe I am correct in saying that this was a 12¾-inch gun, having a cast-iron body reinforced with steel hoops of German manufacture; that it was firing a 760 lb. projectile with the low charge of 170 lbs. of powder, and that it blew the breach out.

With respect to the rapid wearing out of large guns. I wonder to how many of those present, or indeed, to how many of the public who interest themselves in guns, it has occurred, to consider the facts as regards the wear on large guns as compared with that on small guns. Let me show you why it is that the erosive power of the gases per unit of surface, must be so much more in a large gun, than it is in a small one. Let us take, say a 6-inch gun and a 12-inch gun, and assume that the linear dimensions of the 12-inch gun are just double, in all respects of bore, powder-chamber, and projectile, those of the 6-inch gun.

Then obviously the linear dimensions being doubled, the projectile of the 12-inch gun will be eight times as heavy as that of the 6-inch, for the weight will increase as the cube of the linear dimensions, and the powder-charge will also be eight times as heavy, and will produce eight times as much gas. But the area of the bore of the gun will increase only as the square of the doubled dimensions, and will therefore be in the 12-inch gun, only four times the area of the 6-inch; but this area of four times, has to afford passage to the gases of eight times the weight of powder, and thus the rate of erosion is inevitably increased, as the guns become larger and larger. This is an inexorable law, and one to which all guns, whether British or foreign, are equally subject. There is no help for it; but provision can be made, and is made, to render the reparation comparatively simple and inexpensive.

In answer to those who speak as though there were finality in the science of gun construction, and who complain of us for making guns, which are now becoming obsolete; the reason is so obvious that I hardly need to state it. If all other nations would agree to abstain from gun-making, until the perfect gun was discovered, we could do the same, but they will not; they arm with the best weapon of the day, and we must do likewise, although feeling sure that in a few years, that which we are now doing, will be obsolete.

The fact I have brought to your notice, about guns standing their full charges, and similar guns failing under half charges, is an evidence that the guns can as a rule bear the full charge, and that the causes from which they give way, are such as frequently could not be met by a reduction of the charge, and, therefore—for it comes to very much the same thing—could not be guarded against by making our guns stronger; but there are those who say, "Why don't you make your guns stronger? " Why don't you provide a greater margin of safety? Look at " boilers and at railway bridges, and the percentage of extra " strength allowed in these cases." The gun-maker might retort by saying, that neither bridges nor boilers have been found to be absolutely safe, but he would do better to give the true answer, which is this; that the exigencies of the case will not admit of these extra strengths being given, and that of necessity the strains to be endured by the metal in the Big Guns, must be far in excess of those, which could be imposed upon the metal of either bridges or of boilers.

But let us imagine what might happen if we acted on this principle of putting more metal in our guns.

It will be admitted, I presume, that there must be some limit to the weight of artillery, a given size of ship is capable of carrying; having regard to the load of her armour, her machinery, her coals, and her stores. Say, for the sake of illustration, that in some particular ship this weight was 440 tons, and that it was to be used up in four 110-ton guns. Let us take two such ships, one belonging to the enemy, and one to us; the enemy, wo will say, bores up his 110-ton gun to 16 inches, and fires a corresponding projectile with its appropriate energy. Wo, for extreme safety, have determined on boring up our 110-ton gun to only 12 inches, and have thus rendered ourselves incapable of firing more than a 12-inch projectile, or one that weighs but some 43 per cent. of that of our opponent, and if moving at equal velocities, carries but 43 per cent. of the energy. The two ships engage in a combat, with the result that our ship falls a prey to the superior power of the enemy, leaving us, as our consolation, the knowledge that in the fight the enemy had blown the muzzle off one of his 16-inch guns, while all our four 12-inch remain intact, for the benefit of the enemy, however, who has taken our ship.

Let us, as a *résumé*, consider what are the requirements which artillery should meet, and what are the difficulties in the way of satisfactorily meeting those requirements. The first requirement is the power to give high velocity, and accurate direction, to a projectile of such form, that it shall be well adapted to penetrate that which it has to pass through, whether air or armour plate ; and that as regards material, it should be competent to deal with thick armour, having a hard face, and a tough body. These are the results that should be obtained on firing the gun.

With respect to the gun itself, its weight must be kept down, and as a result, its material must bear, both circumferentially and longitudinally, a pressure per square inch, instantaneously applied, far exceeding any pressure, to which similar material is ever exposed, for any other purpose.

To afford facility for safe loading, and for the insertion of a cartridge larger in diameter than the bore of the gun, it must be breech-loading. The breech arrangements must be such that they make an absolutely gas-tight joint, and such that the joint can be rapidly made, and that after having been subjected to the enormous pressure brought on it by the explosion, it must be capable of being as readily unmade, so that the breech may be opened.

To insure the true direction of the shot, the gun must be rifled, and means must be provided, as far as practicable, to neutralise the rush of powder gas and mitigate its erosive effects.

The principal forging for a gun is now of an enormous weight. The ingot, as I have told you, has to be some 66 per cent. heavier than the forging, involving change in composition by the separating out of the carbon while cooling, and involving also the chance of concealed flaws, which no subsequent manipulation can cure. The resulting forging can only be tested for quality in places, and no known, certain, test exists, for concealed flaws. The very act of forging, especially under the hammer, and the act of oil-hardening, are each likely to set up internal strains, the effects of which may be going on for months, and may end in spontaneous rending asunder, as happened with certain cast-iron guns to which I have alluded, and as has happened in more than one instance in the case of steel guns, or of the forgings for steel guns.

The truth is, until some one is found, who can see into the very inside of the metal of the gun, and can do so in every part, and until such a person, even if he could see, possessed the ability by mere inspection to judge of quality, and of condition, no gun can be pronounced absolutely and undoubtedly trustworthy. You may by experience based on experiment, by vigilance in selection of material, by such tests of that material as you can make during manufacture, and by proof of the gun when made, so far diminish the chances of failure, that you are quite prepared to stand beside the gun when fired, as you are quite prepared to take your voyage in an ocean steamer, or to stand alongside a steam boiler; but as in neither the instance of the ocean steamer, nor in that of the steam boiler, can you say with absolute certainty you are safe, so in the instance of the gun, you must be prepared to admit that each time you fire it you run some risk, and you must for the present, be content to find that other nations are in precisely the same condition.

There is an old saying " That bachelors' wives and old maids' " children are perfect." Perfect likewise, are the guns of the critics, and for the same reason, they have no existence ; therefore they have never been fired, and therefore they have never failed.

Just one matter before concluding my remarks about Big Guns and their dimensions, and that is the question of money.

The knowledge needed to make improvements in our guns (so as to keep pace with other nations, as we must, and so as to render them trustworthy), can only be derived from experiment, with the actual guns, projectiles, and armour-plates themselves. Experiments on models will not suffice. To prevent delay in manufacture there ought to be provision for carrying out experiments rapidly. Such provision does not exist. Shoebury is the only important place we possess, and here we enjoy but the partial use ; I say partial, for it is occupied as a school of instruction ; and, moreover, owing to the increase in the size of our guns, the provisions that sufficed in years gone by, do not suffice now. There is wanted a considerable expenditure for the acquisition of a proper extension of the experimental ground.

Again, experiments are delayed because the estimates are cut down, and there is no money available.

Some of you may think experiments should cost very little ; I will ask those who are under that impression, to suspend their judgment, till they consider merely the following instances.

I have told you that hard-faced armour has led to the desire to revert to steel projectiles. I have told you the difficulties there are in producing them, so that they are neither too soft and become deformed, nor are too brittle and are broken up. You will agree with me, I presume, that it would not, having these facts in view, be proper to accept these projectiles without trial, to issue them to the services, and to find when the day of attack came, that they had failed against the enemy's armour-plate. Well, there can be no test short of actually firing against an armour-plate, such as that with which they would have to contend.

Suppose you desire to give an order for several hundred projectiles, say for the 12-inch guns. You must not, if you can avoid it, confine this order to one firm, and especially you must not do so if that firm be a foreign one. You can't expect manufacturers in England, to lay out thousands upon thousands upon special plant, unless you can, from time to time, give them work. Well, this being so, you break up your order into lots, say of 10,000*l.* to 15,000*l.* each—not a despicable order—and you make an agreement with the contractors, that the acceptance of the projectiles shall depend upon certain results being obtained on testing. How can this test, be accomplished? It clearly would not do to agree with the manufacturer, to allow him to send say three sample shots, because if these were accepted as sufficient, there would be no guarantee that the bulk was equal to those which had been prepared as samples, and no inspection, or other test, could satisfy you on this point. What course remains? We know of no other, and foreign Governments know of no other, than to say to the manufacturer, you shall deliver the whole lot ordered of you; there shall be selected from the bulk the three worst projectiles (as far as inspection can guide the judgment) of the lot, and on the result of the firing of these the lot shall be accepted or rejected.

I wonder how many here present have any notion of the cost of carrying out this test. Are they prepared to hear that it cannot be made for as little as 2000*l.*? And I may say that this sum does not allow anything for the wear and tear of the gun, or for the time of the men, and of the officer conducting the experiment.

Assume the test is satisfactorily passed. Even then you have spent over 2000*l.* in ascertaining whether you should, or should not, accept from 10,000*l.* to 15,000*l.* worth of goods. But assume that unhappily the tests are not satisfactorily passed. You have spent your 2000*l.* without any directly useful result to the nation, although with the indirect one (valuable no doubt) of not issuing to the services, untrustworthy projectiles. And while one's primary and all pervading desire, must be the exclusion of untrustworthy projectiles from the services, one cannot but feel deep concern for the manufacturer, who sees the lot of projectiles, which he had made with so much care, and as the outcome of expensive plant, sent to the " scrap heap."

I fear, however, there is no remedy for this expenditure, until some new metallic substance is found, or some process of manufacture of existing materials is reached, which shall enable one to feel so certain of the excellence of the projectiles made of these materials, or prepared by these methods, as to render reception tests unnecessary.

I could, did time permit, give you many other instances of the need of a liberal expenditure on experiments, but I trust I have said enough to cause you to think over the subject, and to believe, that if you wish the nation's means of defence, to be adequately kept up, so as to cope with the means of offence, of those who may " covet" this country, or its possessions, you must be prepared to incur, and even to encourage, a liberal, but useful, and therefore wise, expenditure.

When we consider the mere cost of our fleet and armies in times of peace, involving expenditure upon ships, establishments, small arms, Big Guns, and the experiments connected therewith, are you not prepared to agree with that which I began with? How great the blessings to mankind at large, if nations would cease to covet! but how much more must this truth be impressed upon us, when we consider, not merely the frightful expenditure in time of war, but the loss of life, the misery, and the bar to progress, arising from covetousness! But remember, until nations do cease to covet, a country like England, with its great seaboard, its colonies, and its enormous commerce, must be prepared, as fulfilling the dictates of mere ordinary prudence, to spend annually very large sums; yet, after all, not very large, when considered as Premiums of Insurance for safety.

One word in conclusion; of explanation, and of apology, to the Council and Members of the Birmingham and Midland Institute. When you did me the honour of nominating me your President, I was aware, that it would be part of my duty to deliver an address. I was prepared to find, you might expect, I should discourse on the benefits that such an Institution bestows; that I might, from my position as Chairman of the City and Guilds Technical Institute, have enlarged upon the benefits of Technical Education, and that I might have reviewed the progress you were making, and the progress that was being made throughout the country, and might have congratulated you, and the people of Great Britain, thereon. But these subjects have been rather used up of late, and I found on looking through the list of addresses of your Presidents, that they had selected for those addresses matters having no direct relation to the work of your Institute. I felt tempted to follow their example, and having obtained permission, I thought I could not interest you more than by addressing you on the subject of " Big Guns," for which task, from my position as a Civilian Member of the Ordnance Committee, I felt I had some qualifications. It is a subject of interest in applied science; a subject which I believe is not much understood, although much discussed, and a subject which is undoubtedly of very great national importance.

LONDON: PRINTED BY WILLIAM CLOWES AND SONS, LIMITED.
STAMFORD STREET AND CHARING CROSS.